Curve Balls

(Sam's Adventure)

Rosanna Gartley

A Mouse Gate™ Adventure

Mouse Gate Press
1103 Middlecreek
Friendswood, Texas 77546
281-992-3131 TEL
www.MouseGate.com

ISBN: 978-1-64883-1683
UPC: 6-43977-41683-4

Library of Congress Control Number: 2022940857

FIRST EDITION
1 2 3 4 5 6 7 8 9 10

*Dedicated to my grandson, Sam,
whose love of all things dinosaur
will never be outgrown.*

-Grandma Rosie

Acknowledgments

Thanks to my husband, John for all his help and support and to my publisher, TotalRecall Publications, Inc.

A special thank you to Peyton Schwarz, who assisted with the cover design.

The Book

Sam and his family enjoy a vacation to Disney World where he is thrilled to experience a new ride, The Dino-Soar. This 10- year- old has forever loved everything prehistoric so it's no surprise when he chooses a dinosaur as a souvenir of his trip. Once home, he finds that his keepsake is more than he bargained for. No longer is the plastic figure just a toy. Sam keeps the dinosaur's powers to himself until his elderly neighbor accidently learns the secret. The young boy and the old man have much to learn about each other and their friendship helps both of them make some tough, life-changing decisions.

Chapter 1

By Aleksandra Kolosova

Grandma Terry, known as GT to all who loved her, sat in her swivel rocker with a familiar tool in her hand. She easily threaded the yarn through the eye of the large needle and proceeded to stitch up the sides of the newly knitted sweater. Her calendar showed that her great-grandson, Sam, had a birthday coming up. She couldn't recall just how old he would be but her trusty black book containing all family history would solve that question. GT typically sent cash for birthdays, but she knew just what Sam would love and she had begun knitting it weeks ago. Because it was late August, Sam wouldn't wear his new sweater for several months, but she was sure he would be excited when he saw it. With the last stitch in place, she knotted the yarn then turned the garment right side out and held it in front of her. "This should fit him nicely all winter long," she said out loud with a smile. All she had to do now was to find a box, wrap it up and get it in the mail.

Meanwhile, half-way across the country, Sam woke before his mom had to yell at him to get up for school. These days he was plenty excited because his birthday was tomorrow! Birthdays in their house were big deals. He was sure that after he went to bed tonight streamers would be hung, balloons would be blown up and gifts would be wrapped and placed on the dining room table. No matter how early he got up in the morning, the house would be decorated in his honor. This would all be done in an effort to make him feel special on his big day. He could hardly wait!

With breakfast finished, lunches packed, and bookbags filled, Sam and his older sister, Emily buckled themselves into the backseat for the ride to school. The new school year had begun, and today his job was to count the number of students in his class so his mom could bring in a birthday snack for all to share. The school day zipped by as it usually did, and he could see the family car waiting for him as ran across the playground.

"Hey buddy, how was school?" asked his mom.

"It was good and there are 22 kids in my class," remembered Sam.

"Thanks. I think we should make fruit kabobs and dip for everyone tomorrow. Let's stop at the grocery store on the way home and you can help me pick out the fruits you think the kids would like."

"Where is Em?" asked Sam, suddenly remembering they hadn't picked up his sister at her school.

"She has gymnastics today and then she is going to Victoria's house for dinner tonight. She'll be home in a few hours."

The groceries were carried into the house and placed on the kitchen island. "Take everything out of the bags and place the fruit into the fridge. After supper, we can wash it, cut it up and then you can assemble it onto the skewers. Once the fruit is in the fridge, I need you to run out and grab the mail."

"Okay."

Sam finished with the fruit then turned towards the porch. He slid into his crocs then sprinted to the end of the driveway to the black mailbox. Hiding inside were many white envelopes and other papers. He could already see the grocery store flyer and several other things that looked like junk but then something caught his eye. It was a bright blue envelope and it had his name on it! Then he remembered that tomorrow was his birthday-surely this would be a birthday card. Once back in the house, Sam's excitement couldn't be contained. Half of the mail landed on the dining room table while the other half landed on the floor. If he did notice the avalanche, he paid no attention. All he cared about was the colored envelope he still held in his hand. He didn't wait to use the letter opener nor to ask permission to open it. Recklessly he pulled the envelope apart, tearing most of it but somehow managing to keep the card in one piece. Sam wasted no time opening it to reveal its contents. It was from his, aunts, uncles and cousins in Saskatchewan. Together, they had sent him several gift cards for his favorite places. "Yes! These are awesome!" yelled Sam. What he hadn't noticed was the white, square envelope that had stayed among the business mail. It had landed on the floor, and as he picked it up, he noticed it also had his name on it. The return address was Pennsylvania, USA. "Oh man," said Sam, "I got another card and it's from Papa John and Grandma Rosie."

"Be careful with that one, it probably has a check in it and you won't want to tear it," warned his mom.

"Oh yea, can you open it for me?"

"Sure, bring it here." mom reached for the opener and slid it carefully across the top of the envelope then handed the piece of mail back to her son. Sure enough there was a check inside.

"Yes! I knew it! This will go straight into my bank account."

"Actually Sam, there is one more thing," said his mom as she quickly sifted through the remaining mail. "There is a parcel at the post office for a Sam Muir," she said while holding up the notice card as proof. "I'm guessing it was too big for the mailbox."

"This is the best day ever!" Can we go get it?"

"You can go, just take this card with you. The post office is on the next block. If you go now, you'll be able to make it before they close." Sam didn't need to be told twice. Before he heard the whole sentence, the screen door had slammed shut and he was racing down the driveway towards the street, postal card in hand. The potatoes had just been placed in the pot when Sam came bursting through the back door. He carried a box that had been wrapped in brown paper and secured with a good amount of packing tape. Without a doubt, it was only the sturdy packing tape that had prevented the parcel from already being ripped apart by the birthday boy.

"I need help mom," called out an impatient Sam.

"Just a minute. Let me see what you have there." Sam handed the parcel to his mom. "Did you see who it's from?"

"No, I just grabbed it and ran home."

"Take a look at the return address."

"Wow! It's from GT!"

"So today you got two things from Saskatchewan and one from Pennsylvania. You are very lucky to have so many people who care about you." But the sentiment was lost on the boy who only wanted to see what was in the gift.

"Can I open it?"

"It's not your birthday yet, can't you wait one more sleep? "teased his mom.

"Awe mom, come on. I would really only be opening it a few hours early," reasoned Sam.

"I guess GT wouldn't mind. Here, let me help you. We are going to need scissors." Once the paper was off, Sam took control of the box. The top came off and he found another birthday card and a sweater. He picked up the blue sweater and at first felt disappointed. Clothes weren't much to get excited about. Only Emily cared about that stuff.

"Let me see what you got." Sam picked up the sweater and held it up for his mom to see and it was then that his eyes lit up. Yep, it was a sweater with a huge dinosaur on the front. "I can tell GT knitted it herself."

"How did she know I love dinosaurs?"

"Sam, everyone knows you have loved dinosaurs and everything about them since you were hardly old enough to talk. Dinosaurs and volcanoes! Just ask Grandma Rosie's friend, Maggie. You remember her?"

"Of course, she always found me pictures and videos on her phone; and Grandma Rosie sent me that big book on dinosaurs. Can I wear my new sweater to school tomorrow?

"Uh, I don't think so, buddy. It's too hot for a wool sweater. In a few months it will feel cozy. It looks like GT knows how fast you grow. She made it big enough to fit you for a while."

Chapter 2

By Ssstocker

Creak, creak, creak. Emily woke to the sound of someone walking down the old staircase towards the dining room. She instantly knew who it was and why. Although her eyes were barely open, she could see how dark her room was and that meant no one should be out of bed yet. Forcing herself to sit up, she gave a mighty stretch and threw back the covers. There would be no more sleep for anyone in a minute or two. She knew Sam would be examining whatever was on the dining room table. In no time, he would be ripping off the wrapping paper then there would be squeals of joy. Then whatever it was-likely something noisy, would start up. There would be no more sleep today. Emily slid on her slippers and made her way to the master bedroom. She would make sure she wasn't the only sleep deprived person in the house. After all, whatever noise maker Sam got would not be her fault!

"Hey! Sam's up." Without opening her eyes, Emily's mom responded, "You aren't the only one who heard him."

"You may as well get up. We all know he isn't going back to bed." Unfortunately, Emily made perfect sense so getting up and out of bed was the only option. As they climbed down the stairs, they could hear a jubilant Sam in the dining room. His eyes were as wide as saucers as he continued opening his gifts. It wasn't for several minutes that it suddenly dawned on him that he hadn't yet opened anything from his family. His party would be Saturday and maybe they were waiting until then to give him his present. Suddenly his mom turned to leave the room and instructed Sam to sit down at the table. *Yes!! This must be it!* thought Sam. In no time she was back with a large brown envelope which she put in front of the birthday boy.

"Happy birthday, son. Here is your gift."

Somewhat disappointed and confused, Sam reached for the envelope. *Am I getting too old for real presents?* wondered Sam. He had always received beautifully wrapped gifts although he had never really appreciated the time that went into wrapping them. He slowly picked up his gift, noting it wasn't wrapped or even sealed. The weight of it indicated there were many papers inside. Sam lifted the flap and unceremoniously dumped the contents out onto the table. A handful of colored brochures stared back at him-all with a familiar theme.

"Disney!" Sam screeched, "Are we going to Disney?"

"You bet we are," laughed mom.

"Me too?" asked Emily.

"Of course, all of us."

"When?" asked Sam.

"In about six weeks."

"Only six weeks?"

"Yep!"

"Yes!!" exclaimed Sam. Although Emily couldn't stop smiling it occurred to her that she had never received anything so grand for her birthday.

Six weeks went by quickly helped by the new school year and the resuming of the kids' after school activities. A calendar had been hung in the dining room with a pen attached. Daily, Sam and Emily took turns crossing off the date before they climbed the stairs to bed. Before they knew it, they watched the suitcases being carried up from the basement. Let the excitement begin!

Chapter 3

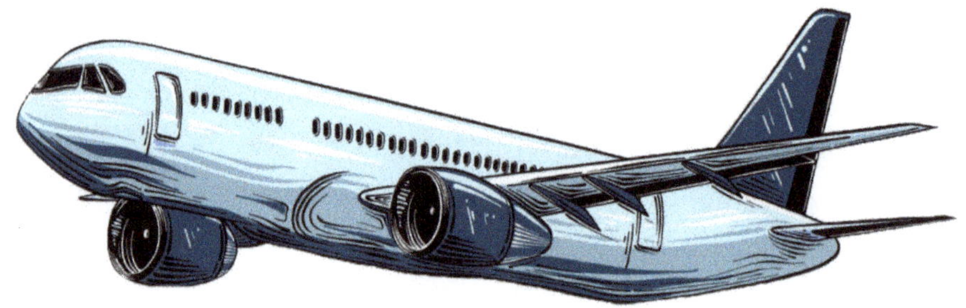

By Andiz

The family had been to Disney World once before and had flown to many Caribbean destinations. But to Sam and Emily flying was still a thrill and of course the theme park itself, was just about the coolest place they could think of. Sam had already spent time on the family's computer looking at the Disney website. He was eager to see if the park had any new attractions and he was especially looking for anything dinosaur related. After landing, they would collect their luggage, pick up their rental car then settle into their temporary home. The house had a pool so they would stay there the rest of the day. Tomorrow they would be at Disney bright and early!

Emily and Sam had different opinions regarding what they should do first. As usual, they had to compromise. It was decided they would alternate days. One day Sam would decide what would be that day's activities and then the next day would be Emily's turn. The grown-ups got to have a say in some activities as well-it was only fair. Day one at the Magic Kingdom was all about Emily. She was able to decide on the day's activities and of course they included some girly stuff and not the least was a complete make-over at the Bippity Boppity Boutique. Sam trailed behind as they entered the huge Disney store that housed the salon. There were more princesses in the place than he could count. Every princess from every Disney movie was represented-only about ten times over! *What do girls see in dressing up in big, poufy dresses, fancy shoes and wearing make-up?* said Sam to himself. Once Emily and his mom were escorted into the boutique Sam looked through the store then headed outside to find something interesting.

Several hours later the two women emerged. Mom looked the same, but Emily had certainly changed. With her new hairdo and full make-up, his sister looked completely different. He had to admit to himself only, of course, that she looked kind of pretty. He would never admit that to anyone else. *Too bad,* he thought, *all that time and money that was spent would float away in the swimming pool later that day.*

Sam was awake early on day two and eager to remind his family of the day he had planned. There were the usual fast and scary rides, meet and greet with some of his favorite superheroes and of course numerous stops where a guy could get some tasty junk food; then eventually lunch at the buffet. Following that, he had planned what he hoped would become his favorite ride ever. It was brand new at Disney and named the Dino-Soar. The description said it was unforgettable. There was also a bonus. Anyone who rode it on its opening day got a gift certificate to the Disney store. Usually Sam hated shopping-for anything, but he had noticed some cool looking dinosaurs in the on-line store and he hoped they would have them for sale in the park too. They were loaded into the second car on the track, secured with the metal bar and then inched along while the remaining cars were filled.

"Come on! Let's go!" said an impatient Sam to no one in particular. His car began picking up speed and the butterflies in his stomach began to fly with excitement. Within seconds, they were in complete darkness when an enormous dino lunged at them from the side. For the few seconds that Sam saw it he thought it was bright green with dark green patches, horns on its head and many rows of scissor-sharp teeth. Sam was too old to be fooled. He knew it wasn't real, but it had made him jump and he felt his heart racing. *Oh yea, this is going to be awesome*, he thought to himself. He was sure that in the car behind him Emily had probably screamed and even peed a little. Girls! Such wimps! Now they were out of the dark, passing through what the earth might have been like in prehistoric times. It looked like he expected it would. He had done lots of reading about dinos and how they lived so he thought the Disney production was realistic. The Disney engineers would have been so relieved to hear this! After several more minutes of twists and turns, in the dark, through a waterfall, seemingly chased by a flying dino the ride concluded. It had been spectacular! Disney had done it again and as they left the car; they were each handed a ten-dollar gift card for the store. Coincidentally, they had to exit the ride through the store.

"How convenient," expressed Sam.

"Yea, how convenient," replied Emily while rolling her eyes.

"Come on guys, I want to spend this."

"No surprise there," said mom. The store was filled with all things Disney but had a section that seemed to co-ordinate with the dinosaur ride. After much consideration, multiple passes through the respective aisles Sam emerged to find the family and show them the loot he soon hoped to own.

"Whatever you want, buddy. You can have my gift card too," said mom. Emily had already exited the store with her new girly treasures.

"Everybody look what I got," smiled Sam while emptying his bag. I got a new backpack and this guy to match." The backpack was dark green in color with a collage of photos taken of different kinds of dinos. Of course, no one had actually been able to take real pics of dinosaurs, but scientists had used bones to determine what they would have looked like. Sam had seen these in several museums and of course had marveled at the animatronic ones in the movies. "Look at this guy!" he demanded while holding up a plastic figure of yet another prehistoric creature. And that's when the Magic happened!

"I saw the bin full of them, why did you pick that one?" asked mom.

"Why did he pick any?" sneered Emily. Sam ignored his sister's sarcasm without responding.

"This one is special. I can't believe they had one. Scientists aren't one hundred percent sure, but they believe the Carnotaurus could change its skin color to blend in with the environment. See how green he is, that's because there were a lot of green plants like trees, ferns and stuff like that where he lived. This species wasn't very big so hiding was important. It was the only way he wouldn't be eaten. They were kind of fast though. Well fast enough to outrun some things. Its tail and its teeth were what some animals had to be careful about."

"Like a chameleon?" asked Emily. Surprised that his older sister even knew what a chameleon was he answered, "Something like that. He was at the bottom of the bin, but I saw him. I guess he isn't very big or well-known, so no one wanted him," suggested Sam, "I'm going to put him into one of the pockets of my new backpack."

"Of course, you will," sighed Emily. She was completely over the dino rollercoaster, the dino store, the dino backpack and dinosaurs in general.

"Let's go eat before the lines get too long," suggested mom. *Now you're talking,* thought Emily.

Chapter 4

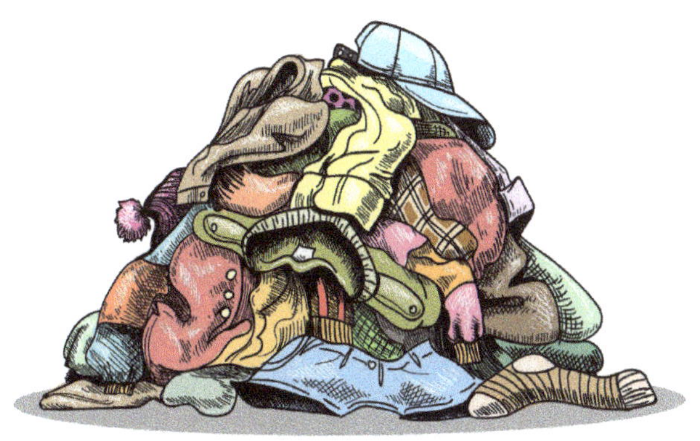

By Vectortatu

The trip to Florida had been a success but tiring for some. The kids, on the other hand, seemed to have boundless energy and stomachs of steel proven by the wacky roller coasters they happily endured and the unending food and snacks they digested. But even the kids admitted it would be good to be home, back to their real life of school, friends, and activities. The kids' hotel room was less than organized so packing was going to take a while. Much to Emily's dismay she had had to share a room with her tornado brother. At home, her room resembled something out of a design magazine. Not only was it beautifully painted, furnished and of course, accessorized but it stayed that way day after day. Emily had put herself in charge of her bedroom years ago. By age five, she knew how to organize her clothes-color coordinated naturally, in her walk-in closet. Before coming downstairs each morning, her bed was made, her curtains opened and her stuffies put in their places all snuggled up to her pillows. She wished she could convince her brother that having a clean, organized room would make his life so much easier. But that was a lost cause so instead all she could do was shut Sam's bedroom door every single time she walked past it. At least if she couldn't see the mess, she could pretend it wasn't there. Emily's room was an example of who she was. Neat, tidy, mature and serious about school. She and her mom were much alike while poor Sam had to be prodded and nagged to keep up with his chores and schoolwork. His personality, however, was charming. Those who could remember the fictional character, Dennis the Menace could see so much of him in Sam. It was with trepidation that his mom would go to parent-teacher interviews each term, yet she always managed to leave with a smile and a happy heart. Yes, his teachers reported that Sam could be easily distracted so focusing was a problem, and he was certainly a social child, in and out of the classroom; no one had more friends than Sam. They also reported that no student cared more about the feelings of the other children than her son. Apparently, he had the biggest heart and smile to go with it. He was also highly intelligent they said. His vocabulary was far beyond his grade level and when he became interested in a subject he would research and learn about it like a college professor. Everyone at school knew about his obsession with dinosaurs and he was known as the school expert on the subject.

Sam hauled his suitcase upstairs to his room and flung it on the bed. Rummaging through it he was only looking for one thing-his new backpack with the dino attached. He quickly found the backpack but the new green dino was nowhere to be found. He began throwing clothes, by the armload, out of his suitcase onto the floor. Finally, near the bottom and off to the side in his luggage was the little guy.

"There you are," said Sam feeling relieved, "For a minute I thought you were lost." He picked up the plastic shape and placed it on a shelf in front of his collection of dinosaur books.

"Sam, please bring down all the clothes from your suitcase, I'll be starting laundry soon," yelled his mom up the stairs. He began gathering up the dirty clothes in his arms dropping a bathing suit on the stairs and a couple of socks while walking through the kitchen. With the car back in the driveway, neighborhood friends knew the family had returned. A knock on the back door was heard and Sam was out the door eager to tell his buddies all about his trip.

Chapter 5

By Ekaterinavasilevskaya1

"Come on, get up Sam," said mom while gently shaking his shoulder. Today it's back to school." Immediately, Sam wanted to roll over and go back to sleep but then he remembered he hadn't seen most of his friends for over two weeks and he had lots to tell them. He threw on some clothes then spotted the new backpack on his desk which reminded him of the new dinosaur. He reached for it, but it was not on his shelf. He was sure he had placed it there yesterday before going outside. He checked on the floor, under the shelf and under his pajamas, which of course, were on the floor. It was nowhere to be seen. Mom began calling for him to come downstairs to eat breakfast, but he had ignored her until he heard the tone of voice that meant business. Emily! Emily must have been in his room and moved or taken his dino.

"Emily! Emily!" Sam shouted while running down to the kitchen. "Where is my new dino? It was on my shelf and now its missing."

"Are you crazy? You think I took it? That would mean I would have to go into your room. I wouldn't go into your filthy room even if I had to. And that stupid toy of yours doesn't interest me at all. Now get out of my way so I can go do my hair." Sam really couldn't argue with his sister. She never went into his room, so he had to admit, to himself only of course, that he had falsely accused her. But where could it be?

"Mom did you find my new dino when you did laundry?"

"No Sam I didn't. but I found two mismatched socks and I presume their mates are somewhere in Florida. Really Sam! I wish you had been more careful when you packed your stuff.

"I only lost two? That's not bad for me. Besides I'll wear those two as a pair, it doesn't matter to me if they don't match," he replied with a toothy grin that made his freckled nose wrinkle.

"It's a good thing you're cute," replied his mom trying to suppress a smile. "Now, get your butt out of here and go brush your teeth. Running a brush through your hair wouldn't hurt either." But the end of her sentence was lost in thin air. Sam had already bounded noisily up the stairs oblivious to his mother's commands. He couldn't take any more time at the moment to continue his search, but it would be a priority once he was home from school.

At school he was the center of attention. He had just returned from one of the best adventures a kid could take. A couple of his friends had been to Disney and were eager to compare notes but most of the kids had only fantasized about the place while watching the ads on television. And

Sam, being the amazing storyteller that he was, took great pleasure in divulging every minute detail. They spied his new backpack and thought the images on it were cool, but Sam knew he had to keep secret the part about his new plastic dino. He was afraid that his buddies would think him too old to be carrying around a plastic toy. He didn't know enough about it yet to share anything with his friends. He knew the name of the species it represented but once he looked it up in his dino book he would learn so much more about it. Then he could show the guys and inform them as to where the dino lived, what it ate, who were its enemies and any special talents it had. That would make it seem less than a kid's toy and more like a scientific relic.

Home from school, Sam's first thought was to find his new toy and read about it. He couldn't get to his room fast enough. He threw his backpack on the bed, opened his curtains and turned on his light.

"That's better," said a small voice. Thinking he had heard something, Sam stopped in his tracks. He listened but all he could hear was the wind outside his window and a car driving past. He knelt onto the rug prepared to crawl under his bed if necessary. Then he heard the voice again. He slowly stood back up careful not to make any noise.

"That's better." This time he knew he had heard a real voice and his heart began to pound. He swung his door shut half expecting someone to be hiding behind it but the only thing he found was a pair of shorts. He then slid open his closet door but again there was nothing in there that could talk. He didn't believe in ghosts, but he did believe in pranking sisters! Surely Emily had concocted some sort of device to annoy and maybe spy on him. Tiptoeing out of his bedroom he ventured down the hall to Emily's room. The door was shut as usual. He wasn't supposed to darken the doorstep of her room, as she put it, but this was war and he was going in. Surely, he would catch her red-handed. Silently, he pushed the door open and jumped back while yelling a very loud, "Aha-caught you!" But the room was disappointedly empty. Even an examination of the closet and under the bed yielded zero results.

"What was that yelling about?" asked mom who was now standing at the bottom of the stairs not looking too happy.

"I thought Emily was home," admitted Sam.

"No, today she has gymnastics."

"Oh yea, I forgot what day it was." So, it wasn't Emily, then who? It must have come from outside. Oh well back to trying to find the dino. He grabbed a flashlight from his dresser drawer and again knelt down on the floor to take a good look under his bed. He didn't like what he saw, several socks that didn't make a pair, a half-eaten bag of chips, his baseball, a yoyo and lots of dust, but no dino.

"Over here." Startled by the voice, Sam turned quickly towards its direction. There was his new toy sitting on the shelf against the books. Instead of going to get it he moved further away, never taking his eyes off of it. "It's okay, I won't hurt anything."

"Are you talking?" responded Sam in a whisper. "But

how, you're made of plastic. I bought you. I have lots of others like you in a box over there."

"Have a seat and I'll explain." Sam was stunned and afraid, too scared to even call for his mom. He did as he was told and sat down on his bed as far away from his new friend as possible. What he really wanted to do was run as fast as he could down the stairs, but his legs were like jelly and he was shaking a little. Instead, he just sat there. His mom wouldn't believe him anyway.

"I don't have all the answers, Sam, but I know a few things."

"How do you know my name?" asked Sam.

"I can hear, everybody calls you Sam, so I figured it's your name."

"You're right, it is my name. Why can you talk?"

"All I know is that it's Disney magic."

"Disney magic? I thought that was just advertising to get people to go there."

"Well, now you know better, Disney magic is real if you are at the right place at the right time."

"How was I at the right place?"

"Remember the new ride?"

"Of course, it was a really cool rollercoaster through prehistoric times."

"Yes, it is new and in a new part of the park. When they excavated the area to build the new coaster, they dug me up. No one saw me because I was so small compared to the buckets of dirt and the huge rocks and trees. But I was there. After that, I don't remember everything, but I ended up in that big plastic bin where you found me."

"You were way down in the bottom, but I knew you were special. Why didn't you talk to me before now?"

"It's a bit complicated. There are a couple of things I need to keep me healthy. I need lots of sunlight and I need limestone. I didn't have much of those in that store. I had a bunch of limestone dust on me from when I was dug up, but I couldn't get any sunlight."

"Then I bought and rescued you."

"Yes, you put me in your shirt pocket, and I got some sunlight. But then the light faded at night, and I got weak. The next morning, the sun came out but then you packed me in the dark to fly home. Once here, you put me on your shelf, and I started to become stronger. But then night came again. You get the picture…" Sam was astonished! A real dinosaur who needed limestone and sunlight?? Was this a freaking dream?? Should he tell someone? He tried to think about who he would tell and what he would say. Then he thought about what news it would be. Scientists would want his dino and take it from him for sure. As if to read Sam's mind the dino pleaded, "Please don't tell anyone about me. I won't last long if they take me and examine me and do experiments on me. I don't want to end up stuffed in some museum." Sam knew enough to know that scientists would probably do all of those things. He had been to many museums, and everyone had the bones of some dinosaur or other on display. No! He couldn't do that to the little guy!

"Don't worry I won't tell anyone cause I think they would take you away."

"Thanks buddy."

"Now what do I do with you?" asked Sam needing some guidance. He now realized it wasn't just a plastic toy souvenir.

"I have no idea but being here is better than being in that bin with all those other toys. Do people really think dinosaurs were like the ones in the store?"

"Sort of. Scientists have found skeletons and put them back together, so we think we know what some of them looked like. I think they are really cool because they come from a different time. I can't imagine what it would have been like back then. With the help of some movies that have been made about dinosaurs I guess we think we know."

"I'd like to see those movies sometime."

"No problem."

"In the meantime, I could really use a bath in some limestone dust."

"Limestone, limestone where do I get limestone?" Then he remembered that there was a very large limestone quarry near the cement plant in a neighboring town. Surely there would be lots of dust. But now he needed to find a way to get to it and collect some. The quarry was too far for him to ride his bike. Sam thought for a minute. He would have to tell a little white lie.

"Mom! mom!" yelled Sam as he flew down the stairs. "Can we go to the cement plant? I need some limestone dust for school."

"Really? Limestone dust?"

"I forgot to bring the note home from school, but I need it for science." This did indeed sound like her son. The first day back at school and he had already forgotten an important note. At least he had remembered he needed the dust. "Can we go now?"

"I suppose so, let's get going before it's dinner time."

"Great!" Sam dug around in the pantry and came up with a good-sized container with a lid. He had no idea how much he should get but he would rather get more than enough. He wasn't sure how the dinosaur would bathe in it but for now the important thing was to get it.

On the way home from the quarry, Sam was busy thinking about many things. He worried about his new friend and whether he could keep him healthy and a secret. The limestone dust would be a life saver and so would the sunshine. His room got light but no real sunshine. He would have to figure out how to get his buddy into the sun. First of all, he needed to find out his name. Yep, when got home that's what he would do. With the container of limestone dust tucked under his arm he raced up to his room. The little dino was pale in color and seemed weak.

"I got the dust," whispered Sam, "What should I do with it?"

"Put me in it, just shove me down."

"How long will it be until you feel better?"

"A few hours, I think." Sam tucked the dino down into the dust.

"What is your name?"

"I don't have one."

"Well, you should have one."

"Okay, I'll leave that up to you." Sam got out his dinosaur encyclopedia that Grandma Rosie had given him and began to look for the section that described the chameleon dinosaur. Surely, he would read something in the information that would help him decide on a great name.

Chapter 6

Following a night buried in the dust, Sam's new roommate appeared stronger.

"Good morning," whispered Sam. It was still dark outside and he wasn't sure if his pal was awake. But then a small voice answered, "Good morning."

"How are you feeling today?"

"Much better inside but very pale outside."

"I know. My room doesn't get any sunlight."

"I can't change color when I'm like this. I'm too faded."

"You mean you can really change color? I read about you, but I didn't know if it was true. The book said that scientists weren't sure about it."

"Oh yes I can match my surroundings like a chameleon," he bragged.

"Oh man! That is so cool! I watched a chameleon in a pet store once-it was awesome!"

"I will be able to do that but first I need a good dose of sunshine."

"I'll take you outside with me today so you can get some sunlight. At least I hope you can, some days are cloudy."

"Even on cloudy days I should be able to get enough rays to help."

"I forgot about that. My mom says that I can get a sunburn even on cloudy days." A gentle knock on his bedroom door startled Sam.

"Time to get up Sammy," said his mom.

"I'm already up." Sam's mom was shocked. She couldn't

remember the last time her son was up and out of bed without being nagged. Oh yes, she could- the morning of his birthday.

After getting ready for school, Sam stopped to think about how he would attach his friend to his bookbag. He couldn't keep him inside a pocket every time he was outside or else the dino would not get much-needed sunshine. He looked around his room and spotted one of his old action figures. The figure had a removable belt around his waist. Sam knew it would fit as a collar on the dinosaur. Then he could use a small carabiner to attach the collar onto a zipper pull of his bookbag. At recess the sun was shining bright and Sam took the dino outside with him. He sat alone on the ground with his back against the playground fence. It wasn't long before the supervising teacher came along.

"Hey Sam, why aren't you out on the soccer pitch with your buddies?"

"I brought my dino book today to do a little reading," said Sam as he pulled a large book from his bookbag.

"Wow! That's a big book, it's got to be two or three inches thick," remarked the teacher.

"Yep, my Grandma Rosie gave it to me. She knows I have always loved learning about dinos." He held it up for the teacher to have a closer look.

"This is not a story book that's for sure."

"No, it's like an encyclopedia except its only about dinosaurs."

"Maybe you could do a presentation to my class sometime. You could talk about your favorite dinosaur."

"I could do that", said Sam rather proudly. He already knew what dinosaur he would talk about. As the teacher moved on he began to thumb through the pages. "Here you are," he said. "This page is all about you." He carefully held up the book for the little creature to see. "It says you are a Carnotaurus.

"That's right, I am."

"Hmmm, I think I'm going to name you Camo."

"I've never had a name before, this is exciting! Why Camo?"

"Because you camouflage yourself to whatever is around you-so Camo it is!"

"I like the sound of it too." The bell rang and Sam followed the other students back into the school building. The bookbag was placed back in its proper cubby with Camo securely attached.

The walk home was unremarkable with Sam and Camo enjoying the bright autumn sun when several boys caught up to Sam.

"Hey Sam, we are going to the lot to play ball-you coming?" Now baseball was one of Sam's favorite things to do. He loved to pitch, catch, play on base, play in the outfield or the infield. He would play anywhere but of course he loved batting best.

"Yep, just let me dump off my stuff first and change my clothes." He ran into the house and charged upstairs making as much clatter on the stairs as a team of horses.

"Sam, slow down, there's no fire," instructed his mom.

He shed his clothes for jeans and a t-shirt then turned to Camo, "What should I do with you?"

"I could use some dust." With that, Sam carefully unclipped his friend and placed him in the container of limestone dust.

"I'll see you later and have a good rest." He pounced down the stairs two at a time, ran through the dining room and stopped near the back door to scoop up his ball cap and glove. The 'lot' as the kids called it was earmarked for a lovely park and playground. Unfortunately, the town had not yet raised the significant amount of money necessary to build the green space. It was a large area, exactly a block square covered in weeds and quack grass. The town's maintenance crew mowed it weekly and the neighborhood kids had claimed it as an unofficial ball diamond, soccer pitch, football field, shinny rink or whatever else they needed it to be depending on the game choice of the day. And until winter set in it would be used almost exclusively for baseball. The back of Sam's yard was only separated from the lot by a six- foot fence. Senior housing backed onto the other three sides of the lot. The seniors lived in long low buildings with each building having ten units, allowing for 30 units surrounding the field. Each unit had a backyard that faced the lot, and it wasn't unusual for many of the older citizens to sit in their backyards and watch the children play. Sometimes they would shout encouragement, clapping at a good play or chastising the kids if foul language erupted, or tempers got out of hand. Sam didn't know any of their names and the seniors didn't know many of the kids either, although they enjoyed watching the kids grow up as the years went by. There was little contact between the young and the old but on

Halloween most of the kids visited each senior unit as it was so easy to get lots of treats in a very short amount of time.

Today, Sam was one of the last to get to the lot. There was a mix of grade schoolers, middle schoolers and a few high school students; athletic and not so athletic, boys and girls. A number of younger girls were skipping together near one corner, but a few were ready to play ball once teams were picked. The unwritten rule said the oldest two to show up were team captains and a flip of a coin decided who got first pick. Everyone was familiar with the ritual and no one griped about it or wanted it changed. Sam knew he would be picked soon. He wasn't one of the oldest or biggest, but he had a good arm for throwing and could catch a ball. The game would go on until some parent broke it up for supper or it got too dark to play. These days going home to eat was usually what ended it and it was common for Sam's mom to yell at him over the fence which usually alerted the other kids to check their phones for the time and head home themselves. And that is what happened on this day. Sam kicked off his dusty shoes at the door although his white socks were not much cleaner than his shoes. He threw his cap and ball glove into his cubby and proceeded straight to the bathroom to wash up. Something smelled really good and if he had to guess he would say it was spaghetti sauce. The table was set and the food was being transferred to the table. Uncharacteristically, instead of plopping down on his chair and digging in he ran upstairs two steps at a time.

"Sam! Where are you going? Supper is ready." Sam had

to think fast-what would his mother believe?

"I need to change my shirt first; this one is filthy from sliding into second." Although it would have been a reasonable response from Emily, Sam didn't typically care about his appearance, particularly his clothing-clean or otherwise.

"What is with this kid?" said his mom to herself out loud. Sam of course, had gone upstairs to check on Camo.

"You there, Camo?"

"Of course, I'm here."

"Okay good. You doing alright?"

"Yea, I'm feeling better now."

"Look I gotta go and eat, I'll be back later." Then as he was bounding out of his room, he remembered his shirt. He whipped it off throwing it on the floor and grabbed the first one he saw in his drawer and headed for the dining room.

Chapter 7

By Maryna Kriuchenko

Every day Sam clipped Camo to his bookbag and off to school they went. Only during lunch would Sam take the dino and bookbag outside for some light. Taking his bookbag outside during recess would have raised questions, so when the recess bell rang, he cautiously clipped his friend to his belt loop while he played soccer or ball while the dinosaur was able to get the much-needed light. Because of his unique chameleon-like ability he was able to blend in with whatever Sam was wearing and no one ever noticed he was there. After school if he didn't have karate, Little League or swimming lessons, he would stop at home briefly to get rid of his school stuff then zip out the back gate to the lot.

The lot was crowded almost every day. Although no one officially talked about it, everyone knew the sport of the season was changing. Soon ball gloves and bats would be exchanged for hockey sticks and tennis balls. Eventually toques, warm parkas and woolen gloves would replace shorts and t-shirts as the uniform.

The change in seasons brought changes in the weather patterns too. Some days the clouds were so thick Camo was unable to get any rays of sun at all while Sam enjoyed playing. On those days, Sam had to venture to the lot with his buddy hidden often at odd times depending on when the clouds thinned. This had happened several days in a row. Sam had opened the gate, walked into the lot and sat on the ground by himself with his back against his fence. Sam was certain no one had seen him. But he was wrong. Not only did the old man have an interest in watching the local kids play sports, particularly baseball, but he had been a keen bird watcher for decades. The trees and shrubs in the area provided homes for many types of birds. Once the kids left the lot and there was quiet again in the grassy space many of the birds would return to their nests which provided him with some interesting bird watching opportunities. That was how he spotted Sam on several late afternoons.

The elderly neighbor had been spying on a beautiful male cardinal which happened to come to rest on the gate only a couple feet above Sam's head. As he followed the bird's path with his binoculars, he saw Sam sitting alone and seemingly talking to himself. At first, he thought the boy must be speaking into a cell phone but upon further inspection he was sure there were no devices nearby. Although the boy wasn't crying, he didn't look too happy either. Being it was none of his business, the old gentleman shrugged his shoulders and continued following the red bird. As the days wore on, he began to look for the young boy sitting all alone. Sure enough, several days in a row,

Sam was spotted in the same place apparently talking to no one. One day the old man decided to walk over and introduce himself. Sam saw a man who looked to be heading his way. He couldn't take the chance of anyone seeing Camo, so he quickly ducked back through the gate into his own yard. He hoped Camo had had enough sun because once back in the yard he would need to make sure he was hidden. The neighbor was a little perplexed by Sam's behavior. He hadn't meant to scare the child but perhaps his approach had nothing to do with the child's departure. Sam quickly entered the house then cautiously peered through the corner of the mud room window. He was relieved that the old man had not followed him into his yard. He just couldn't get caught with Camo.

Day after day, as the evenings became longer it became increasingly difficult to find full sunlight. Whenever possible, Sam scooted through the gate to sit alone in the lot with Camo exposed to the sky. At the same time each day, the old man was often out in his yard, usually with his binoculars. He continued to see Sam and once or twice thought he saw something move near the boy. Whatever it was, it was small. He assumed it must be a small pet and soon the old man was not only watching for songbirds but also for harmful predators. He didn't need his binoculars to see the hawks circling the lot below. The birds of prey were looking for field mice and garter snakes but whatever pet the boy had might be fair game. Sam was intently listening to Camo and failed to see his neighbor approaching. Before he could hide his dinosaur, the old man loomed over them. Not only had he seen the dino move but he had heard it speak! The boy and the man simply stared at each other, both in a state of shock.

"Hi," said the man.

"Hi," replied Sam as he slowly moved Camo out of sight.

"Hope I didn't scare you,"

"A little. I didn't see you coming."

"Sorry about that. I've seen you sitting alone somedays, thought you looked kind of sad. Everything okay?"

"Sure, no problem. I was just wasting time before supper. If I sit inside my mom will nag me about my homework." The old man chuckled.

"Pretty clever I'd say. Well, I live just over there. Thought I'd come over and say hi. See you later. Say, I've watched you play ball, you're pretty good." And with that the stranger began walking back to his home. Suddenly, Sam heard a loud whistle. He knew it was Emily signaling him to get home to eat.

"Hope you got enough light, Camo. Time to go in."

"I feel good," he replied. Sam pocketed the little guy, went home and let the door slam behind him.

The weather was great for late fall and the lot reflected that. A group of kids played kickball, but most were on or near the make-shift ball diamond. Once the teams were made, some kid with a cast on his right arm yelled "Play ball!" Obviously, he was the designated umpire. Today, the teams were evenly mixed. It would be an interesting game. Although no one got anything except bragging rights if they ended up on the winning team, each kid played their best after all their reputations were on the line. On Sam's third time up to bat, he was facing a full count. The next pitch could determine his fate. The ball was pitched and Sam watched it coming towards him and heard a 'thwack' as it slammed into the catcher's mitt.

"Strike!" yelled the ump.

"That was no strike, it wasn't even close to being across the plate."

"It's a strike!" the ump insisted.

"That's a ball," argued Sam. Then the ump turned to look at someone across the field. The someone gave him a nod and the ump fired back, "See, I told you so!" Sam looked in the direction of the nod. It was the old man who had been sitting in his lawn chair watching their game.

"What does he know?" demanded Sam.

"Oh, he knows!" replied the ump. Sam could see that he wasn't going to win the argument and to make matters worse, the older boys on his team did nothing to support or argue for him. Dejected, he made his way back to the space behind the imaginary third base line dragging the bat behind him.

"You could have told that ump a thing or two," said Sam to a high schooler sitting on the ground cracking sunflower seeds.

"Nope," said the kid without even looking up. "Once Shuck makes a call, that's it, and he signaled that it was a curve ball that fooled you."

"That ump doesn't know anything more than we do," insisted Sam.

"Shuck isn't the ump."

"Then who is Shuck?"

"He's that old man sitting in the blue lawn chair over there."

"So why does he get to decide?"

"I guess you don't know about him."

"So, who is he?"

"He's Shuck. He was a major league baseball player back in the 60's and 70's. He knows his stuff. That's why he gets to decide."

"What? A real ball player?"

"You should talk to him sometime. He's really cool." Then it dawned on Sam that it was the same old man that had snuck up on him days ago. He had talked to a real live major leaguer and didn't even know it. It was a little easier for Sam to accept the strike call now. He couldn't help but keep looking at the man for the rest of the game.

A shrill whistle alerted Sam that supper was on the table. The ball game was over anyway and Sam ran into the house excited to tell his mom about Shuck. "Mom, mom, where are you?"

"In the living room."

"Mom, there's a guy named Shuck that was a real live baseball player and he watched me play ball today."

"Oh really?" said his mom trying to sound interested.

"Yes, he was watching us play and he called me out cause he said the pitch was a strike and I really complained because I didn't think it was and I thought Jason, the ump, was blind but then Matt said it wasn't Jason that called it a strike, that Shuck did. So, I said who the heck is Shuck and Matt said he used to be a ball player. But now he lives in one of those little houses for old people. He often watches us, but I had no idea who he was and that he used to be famous."

"Whoa, Sam slow down."

"Did you know about him, mom?"

"I don't know. What house does he live in?"

"Umm, it's the white one with, I don't know some other color on it too. It's on the right side of the lot about halfway down."

"Oh yes, that's Burt and Nella. I sold their big house for them a few years ago so they could move into one of the senior cottages."

"You mean you've known a major leaguer all this time and you didn't tell me?"

"Sam, I had no idea what he had done for a living. He had been retired for many years before I met him. His career never came up. You called him Chuck?"

"No, not Chuck, its Shuck! I don't know why but that's his name."

"You seem pretty excited about this guy. Why don't you talk to him sometime?"

"I did talk to him one day. I was sitting at the lot and he saw me and came over and said 'hi'. Oh my god! Now I remember, he said he had seen me play and said I was a good player. Oh my god! A real ball player thinks I'm good!"

"Wow! You've had quite a day! I'm sure Burt would enjoy talking with you again."

"Oh no, mom, I couldn't possibly talk to him-he's famous!" mom smiled to herself, she had never seen her son star-struck. It was endearing.

"Maybe he could give you some baseball tips." Sam hadn't thought of that. He could use some coaching especially about curve balls, but he couldn't possibly ask him.

Chapter 8

By Glowonconcept

The weekend came and organizing a ball game on the lot was never assured. Families had plenty of other things to do on Saturdays and Sundays which often included their kids. Sam had been grocery shopping with his mom and Emily and then dragged on several other errands before returning home. He carefully dug Camo out of the dust and slid him into his pocket. He wanted to head over to the lot to give the dino some sun. He grabbed his ball and glove on the way out the door so his mom would think he was going to play ball. As predicted, there were very few kids hanging out on this Saturday morning. Most were girls lingering in a small group, focusing on other stuff besides wanting to play sports. Sam carefully sat on the ground then cautiously took Camo out of his pocket and gently placed him in front of him for some sun exposure.

Meanwhile, Shuck was once again bird watching with the high-powered binoculars that hung around his neck. Fall was here and many birds were flocking to head south for the winter. He really enjoyed learning about his flying friends and their habits. Most days he was unable to stray far from home and watching the birds was something he could do from his backyard. When he wasn't bird watching, he could sit outside and watch the neighborhood young people enjoying various outdoor activities. But today was Saturday and the lot would be quiet. Shuck saw the young boy he had watched play ball the day before and he also recognized him from the brief meeting earlier in the week. He trained his binoculars on the lad and once again, he seemed to be talking to someone although there was no one else nearby. Shuck kept watching and then saw something move on the ground near the boy. It was small, perhaps it looked like a salamander or maybe a pet gecko? It was a little hard to tell so he decided to take a quick walk over and meet the kid's pet.

The sun had finally come out in full force, making it necessary for Sam to pull the brim of his cap down over his eyes. Because of that, he didn't notice the tall gentleman walking straight towards him. Shuck had come close enough to get a good look at the talking dinosaur. Although seldom at a loss for words, the old man could only look and stare. By then, Sam had seen the shoes stop in front of him but by the time he tried to cover Camo it was too late. He quickly stood up with the dino held loosely in his closed hand. Sam's reaction prompted Shuck to respond. "What the heck is that?" he asked pointing to Sam's fist.

"It's just a toy."

"Wow! It sure is lifelike and I thought I heard it talking. Can I see it?" Now Sam didn't know what to do. If he said no, that would be suspicious, but he didn't know what would happen if he opened his hand for the man to see. It seemed clear that Shuck had seen the dino, watched it move and heard it talk. Sam couldn't think of a believable cover story so he simply uncurled his fingers and let Camo rest in his palm. By now, Camo had changed to the color of Sam's skin but there was no hiding from the man who stood only a foot away. "Is that some kind of iguana?"

"Aah, no." Although Sam was tempted to lie his way out, something told him it would be better for him to just tell the truth.

"Can I see him?" asked Shuck, holding out his hand.

"Yes," said Sam as he placed Camo in the old gentleman's palm.

"If it isn't some kind of lizard, then what is it?"

"It's a dinosaur," admitted Sam.

"I know it can't really be a dinosaur, but it sure looks like one."

"It really is one," insisted Sam.

"C'mon buddy, what is it really?" Now Camo had heard enough.

"I really am a dinosaur, believe it or not!" The old man was startled and pulled his hand away as if holding something hot. Camo lost his balance but managed to cling onto the cuff of the old man's sweater so as not to topple to the ground. At the same time, Sam lunged to save his buddy from a tragic fall. There was no damage done to

Camo, but Shuck looked like he might faint.

"Wow! This is incredible. I've heard and read about animatronics but never saw the technology this close up." Sam knew that animatronics were what movie studios used to make dinosaurs and other creatures appear life-like when really, they were controlled by computers. He could have agreed and let Shuck believe Camo was a machine but for some reason he needed to share the truth about his incredible friend. It had been very difficult not to show off a real dino to his friends or to ask for help from his mom to care for Camo. He felt he could trust Shuck and it just seemed easier to share the story than to keep lying.

"If I tell you the truth about my dinosaur, will you keep it a secret?"

"Of course," said Shuck smiling a little at the seriousness of Sam's expression.

"This could take a while. Can we sit together somewhere?"

"Let's walk over to my place. We can sit in the backyard. I should be getting home anyway." The two made the quick walk to Shuck's backyard where he offered Sam a chair. "Just give me one minute to check on my wife." A few minutes later Shuck returned to the backyard with two colas. "Now let's hear your story, young man. By the way, my name is Shuck."

"I'm Sam. My mom said she sold your house before you moved here."

"Oh, was that your mom? It's a small world and it's good to meet you, Sam." Sam sat up straighter in his chair and began, "Well here goes. This is how I found Camo-that's his name, Camo, because he can camouflage himself like a chameleon."

"I see," said Shuck. And while they sipped their pop, Sam explained in fine detail, how he and Camo came to be acquainted. Every now and then, the dino would interrupt with his version of events or to add something that Sam had left out. By the time Sam and Camo had quit talking, Shuck was completely flabbergasted. He didn't want to believe the kid, yet the proof sat right in front of him on his patio table. Sam had summed it up as Disney Magic and the old man could not argue. As Sam finished explaining, he added, "Now you promised me you wouldn't tell anyone-right?"

"You don't have to worry; my lips are sealed." He most certainly wouldn't be telling anyone for two reasons. One, no one would believe him anyway and two, they would think he had lost his mind. No, the boy needn't worry about him spilling the beans. Sam felt good about sharing the story. He had explained how his family had gone to Disney and how he loved dinosaurs since he was little. He explained how important it was to make sure Camo had sunshine and limestone dust at the right times. Camo tried to explain how he felt when he ran low on light and dust. He also remembered to tell why he didn't need to eat anymore because most of his body systems had gone dormant during the millions of years he had laid beneath the surface of the earth.

The patio door opened and an old lady stood there looking at them. She had uncombed hair, a loose dress on, pink slippers and was leaning on a walker. She tried to speak but little came out. Shuck stood up quickly and reached the open door before she could take a step outside. "Nella, you need warmer clothes on if you want to come out. It's chilly out here." The old lady made no attempt to join them-she just stared blankly at Sam. "I better get her back where it's warm. We'll get together again soon, Sam, thanks for the curve ball." That was his cue. Sam stood and scooped up his little friend, pushed his chair up to the table, drained the remaining pop and said good-bye to his host. They left Shuck's yard with Camo clasped gingerly in Sam's hand.

"I wonder what Shuck thinks now. I guess I did throw him a curve ball," pondered Sam.

"What is a curve ball?" asked Camo.

"Well, in baseball, it's a ball that looks like it's been pitched straight, easy to hit but just when you go to swing, it curves, and you miss it. But when people say it and they aren't talking baseball, it means you thought something was one thing, but it turns out to be something different. I think Shuck means he thought you were a toy, but you ended up to be something completely different."

"It will be interesting to talk with him again," said Camo. As they entered Sam's yard, Camo was clipped onto his belt loop. Sam was hungry and he walked into the kitchen looking for a snack.

Chapter 9

Sam couldn't quit thinking about his encounter with Shuck and Shuck couldn't help thinking about his encounter with Camo. The old man had googled many things about finding dinos but of course every site only talked about finding skeletal remains, or unhatched eggs. There was some information written about dinos that could change their color to blend in with their environment; certainly, a clever survival skill. These dinosaurs had a name, but it was too long and scientific for Shuck to remember. It seemed that Sam, if it were true, had made one of the most remarkable finds of the century. He needed to convince the boy to contact the local university. Sam wanted to get back together with Shuck because of baseball. He had also been googling, but not about Camo. He had tried to find out who Shuck was, but he didn't know much more than his nickname and his first name. He needed to know more so he could look through his baseball cards. He hadn't collected too many himself but his uncles, Ryan and Graham, had given him their collections.

After school, the lot was busy with kids. They had to convince some young kids to join in order to have enough for two ball teams. Both teams sucked and after only a few innings, every player threw in the towel and the teams disbanded. Sam decided to head over to Shuck's and see if he was home. Camo was tucked away in his bed of dust up in Sam's room and supper wouldn't be ready for a while. He walked over to the senior's cottage but was unsure about which door to knock on. The only one he could get to without first walking around all the connected cottages was the sliding glass door overlooking the backyard. Although there was no doorbell, surely someone would hear him knocking reasoned Sam. His knock was answered by a lady in medical scrubs. When he asked for Shuck, the lady seemed puzzled. Then he remembered that Shuck had a real name. "I mean Burt."

"Oh yes, he's here, just a minute." The lady disappeared and Shuck came to the door.

"Hello Sam. Come in, come in," beckoned the older gentleman, smiling. "I'm so glad you came over. Follow me, let's have a seat in the living room." Sam politely followed his host and sat down in one of two swivel, rocking chairs. Shuck crossed the room and settled into a barrel chair that was just his size. Although Sam couldn't see anyone else, he could hear voices from down the hall. "The nurse is with my wife," offered Shuck as if he had read Sam's mind.

"Is she sick?" asked Sam, who immediately regretted asking such a nosey question.

"She fell a couple weeks ago and got scraped up pretty good so the nurse changes her bandages."

"Oh," said Sam, not knowing what else to say.

"How about a pop?"

"Sure." This was a treat as Sam wasn't allowed much pop at home.

"Were you and the others playing today in the lot?"

"No, not really. There weren't enough kids to have two decent teams. I'm wondering why your name is Shuck." Immediately, Sam felt embarrassed. He hadn't meant to come right out and ask, it had kind of slipped out.

"You know it's only a nickname?"

"Yes, my mom said your name is Burt and your wife's name is Nella."

"That's right. Your mom has a good memory. It's a nickname I got when I played ball. You know many players chew sunflower seeds. Well, I preferred shucking peanuts in the dugout."

"One of the kids told me you were a major leaguer!"

"I sure was! I played in the majors for eleven years. I was traded a few times and I enjoyed every team I played on. I never received any major awards, but I loved the game-still do. I made a good living and some very special friends that I still keep in touch with. It's been a great life!"

"Wow! You were a major leaguer! I'm hoping I have your baseball card." Shuck laughed, "Well, son, it was a job, a job I loved but contrary to what some believe, we are just regular people. After I retired, I umpired Little League and I enjoyed that almost as much as playing myself."

"Hey, I play Little League."

"I don't ump anymore, too hard to crouch down, my knees don't like it and my eyesight isn't as good as it used to be. I've been to a few local games, but I can't leave the house much anymore because of my wife. The doctors say she has dementia which means she can't remember much anymore. Most days she doesn't know who I am and she seems to be forgetting our daughter too." Sam could see the sadness in Shuck's face.

"You have a daughter?"

"We do, her name is Bonnie and we have two

granddaughters. They are both in college now."

"Do they like to play ball?"

"No," laughed Shuck, "They never picked up a ball or glove that I know of. Our daughter was a swimmer and the girls both swim in college and are into gymnastics. With their studies they are very busy. Maybe someday I'll have great grandchildren that I can play ball with."

"I'll play ball with you."

"One of these days I'll dig out my old glove and we can play catch a while." Sam's eyes lit up. He was going to play catch with a real major leaguer. "We may have to play in the yard because of Nella. I must keep an eye on her when she is awake because she still remembers that she used to cook and sometimes she tries to use the stove which of course is very dangerous. I also worry about her getting outside and walking away, she would never know how to get home." Sam hadn't heard of anyone like that before. It sounded terrible, kind of like having to babysit his wife, but of course he wouldn't say that to Shuck.

"I'll play wherever," said Sam. He could hardly contain his excitement, but it would be up to Shuck to tell him when. He knew they were going to be good friends.

Chapter 10

Shuck sat in his backyard watching the kids play ball. The autumn sun was out and the sky was absolutely cloudless. What a treat to only have to wear a sweater. He found himself watching Sam more than anyone else. He was surprised by the amount of game intelligence the young boy showed. Being able to catch, throw and bat were important aspects of the game but being able to anticipate, remember each opposing player's style and have a clear plan depending on the next play were hard skills to teach and were usually just things a great player was born with. Sam seemed to have been born with them all. Yes, this kid could have potential, he would enjoy mentoring him. Shuck's thoughts were interrupted by a ringing phone. He had forgot, again, to bring his cell phone out of the house. Now the land line was ringing. By the time he got off his chair, walked across the patio and into the kitchen, most callers would have hung up but this time the phone continued to ring. He knew the patient caller must be his daughter, Bonnie.

"Hello."

"Hi dad, you must have been outside."

"Yea watching the kids play ball."

"It sure is great weather to sit outside. Is mom napping?"

"Yes, I tucked her in about twenty minutes ago."

The nurse called me today to say that mom's bruises are healing but that scrape still looks pretty raw. I'm wondering if you think it's painful for her."

"During the day she seems alright but at night she is very restless and favors that side."

"Did you get much sleep last night, dad?"

"Well, I don't know. I guess I was up a few times with her."

"I think it's time we had a talk about placing mom in long term care."

"No! I can still look after her. Nothing much has changed since the last time we had this conversation."

"Yes, dad, I know you can look after her but it's getting too hard on you. At your age you need your rest. You need to worry about yourself too."

"I'm fine. I can't do that to her. She hardly knows me anymore. Imagine how it would be for her in a completely strange environment with no one she recognizes."

"My heart breaks for her too. But I need you to stay healthy. I don't want to lose two parents too soon."

"I know what you are saying but I have to go. I think I hear her stirring." The conversation was going where he didn't want it to go. She had brought up a nursing home for Nella and he wanted no part of it. Shuck hung up the phone abruptly-partly out of necessity so he could check on Nella, but mainly to put an end to the uncomfortable conversation. He wished it were that easy to end the discussion, but he knew he would be forced to discuss nursing homes again. He walked down the hall to Nella, she was sitting up on the side of the bed.

"I thought I heard the baby. Thank you, Burt for getting up with her," said Nella. Of course, there was no baby anymore. Their only child was nearing 50 but so often Nella lived in the past.

"That's okay dear, would you like to get up and sit with me on the patio?"

"Don't you have to work today?"

"No, today I can spend it all with you," answered Shuck as he lovingly took her hand and walked her to the patio, "I'll get your sweater, it's a bit chilly out there." He draped a warm sweater over her shoulders and sat on the chair next to her.

"Nella, do you see that young boy over there in the red ball cap and yellow shirt?"

"Oh, oh that one?" asked Nella pointing towards the ball field.

"Yes, his name is Sam. I think he is rather good for a ten-year-old. And he is a nice young man, too. I think he is worth spending some baseball time with. One of these days, I'm going to do a little coaching." Nella stayed silent, watching the children play. The ball game ended and although Sam noticed Shuck on his patio, he knew it was time to go straight home. He was starving and he needed to check on Camo. He sprinted up the stairs to his room to find Camo still buried in the dust.

"You, okay?"

"I'm not sure. I'm not feeling too good. Maybe because of no sun."

"Let's get you out in the sun. Climb into my pocket."

"You'll have to help, I'm too tired." Sam picked up the little guy and placed him in the pocket of his pants. Just as the screen door was closing, he heard his mom.

"Where are you going? It's supper time."

"I'll be right back in about 10 minutes." Before she could respond, he was long gone out the back gate, slamming it behind him. "Okay, Camo, here is some sun." With help he climbed out of Sam's pocket and turned his body to the sun. He closed his eyes, breathing in the rays if such a thing was possible. After about eight minutes, Sam asked if he was feeling better.

"No." answered Camo, "I don't feel any different." Sam didn't know what to do. Camo needed to stay in the sun, but Sam needed to get to the house as promised.

"I'm going to leave you out here in the sun. But remember it will be sunset before long. I'll come back for you as soon as I can." Reluctantly, Sam went back to the house, leaving Camo propped up against the fence. He consumed supper as fast as he could without raising suspicion. He helped clear the table as instructed and when he was sure there would be no further excuses as to why he couldn't leave the house, he bolted. He flew across the yard and opened the back gate. Sitting just where he had left him was Camo. Now he was brown, just like the fence, a good sign the sun had helped. "You are looking better."

"I feel a little better but after this much time in the sun, I should feel great."

"Any idea why you aren't?"

"The only thing I can think of is that the limestone dust and the sun aren't quite the same thing as being buried in limestone, like I was before being dug up."

"But you've got the dust."

"I know, Sam, it's not your fault. You take great care of me." Now Sam was worried that his current care would no longer be able to keep his buddy healthy. He had no idea what could help.

"The sun has nearly set. We might as well go inside." He placed his friend back into his pocket and went home with the hope that tomorrow would be a better day.

Chapter 11

By Alexmillos

Sam spent most of the night lying in bed worrying about his friend. Camo couldn't sleep either. He was too worried about his life in the 21st century.

"You awake, Camo?"

"Yes."

"I'm worried about you-any idea about what's going on?"

"I keep thinking about it and I'm worried that my genetic make-up won't let me live here."

"What do you mean?"

"When I was born and grew up the earth was very different. I only remember seeing lots of trees and plants. Water had lots of living things in it and of course many kinds of dinosaurs. There were no people, no cars, no planes, no factories or anything else that there is on earth today. Maybe it's all these changes to the earth, the sun, the water and the air that are making me sick." Sam hadn't thought about any of that, but he should have. He had read many books about dinosaurs and the times they lived in. He couldn't believe he hadn't thought about all what Camo had just said.

"Tell me about life when you were young."

"There were thick jungles everywhere with so many kinds of plants and trees. I was much bigger than I am now". Camo's change in size was another thing Sam should have thought about. Every picture he had ever seen of dinosaurs had showed them from large to gigantic to ginormous.

"I know I've shrunk while being buried for millions of years. I was one of the lucky ones. Most dinos my size were eaten by bigger ones."

"You mean hunted and eaten?"

"Of course. Nature lets the healthier, stronger and faster survive. The weak or slow ones are eaten to keep the stronger ones strong."

"I guess that is still how it works in nature. We keep pets safe no matter how weak or small."

"No pets in the dino era," remarked Camo, "you either ate what you could, or you got weak and were eaten."

"Didn't your parents protect you?"

Camo laughed, "I know it's hard for you to understand how it was but dinos don't grow up in families. There is no 'dad' and once I was hatched, my mother was too worried about staying alive herself to worry about me. I grew quickly and I was stronger so I could avoid trouble. The T-Rex's were a problem. They ate everything they could catch which was just about everything. They were so big and so fast. The raptors were another problem. They flew so they could see everything from above, it was so hard to hide from them."

"So, you managed to avoid getting eaten or hurt for a long time."

"Yes, I was very lucky but then the earth changed and I was eventually buried." Hearing this made Sam sad. Camo had lived during a very dangerous time and survived all his predators. But here he was, on earth in the 21st century and it seemed to be making him sick. Sam was afraid he would die.

"I don't know what to do to make this better," admitted Sam, "I think I'll talk to Shuck about it." By afternoon, rain had settled in so no one would be at the lot to play. Sam saw it as a good opportunity to pay a visit to Shuck for some advice. He yelled back to his mom as he opened the back door, "I'm going to a friend's; I'll be back for supper." Sprinting across the lawn to the back gate allowed him an escape without being questioned. He had wanted to bring Camo with him but his dino friend wanted to stay buried in his dust. Once again, he was feeling weak. Sam made it to Shuck's in record time. He knocked on the patio door and this time a different lady answered. "Is Burt here?"

Instead of answering, the lady yelled behind her, "Dad, you have company." Sam could hear Shuck walking towards him from down the hall, his slippers shushing on the hardwood floor.

"Well, hello young man," said Shuck, obviously pleased to see his young friend. "What are you up to today?" Sam noticed the lady who had let him in was still in the room. Shuck followed Sam's gaze and saw his daughter. "Bonnie, dear, this is Sam, one of my neighbors. It was Sam's mother who was our realtor when we sold our house. Sam, this is our daughter, Bonnie."

"So, this is the girl that never played ball," thought Sam immediately. But of course, he wouldn't have dared say it.

"Hi Sam, it's nice to meet you."

"Hi," said Sam unsure of what else to offer. It seemed that Bonnie was pleased that her father had a visitor and turned around and headed down the hall.

"She drops in often," said Shuck, "She is very concerned about her mother and me and likes to keep an eye on us." Sam couldn't tell by his tone if Shuck was pleased or annoyed by her visits. He really didn't want to know so he brought up the reason for the visit.

"I came to ask you about Camo."

"How is our friend doing?"

"Not any better. I've given him lots of sun and he practically lives in his dust now, but it only helps for a little while. I don't know what else to do."

"That's a tough one, Sam, I hate to say it, but our friend isn't from here or even this millennium. I'm afraid the earth now may not be compatible with his body systems like his heart and lungs. Maybe there isn't anything you can do; I know this is quite a curve ball. What does he think?"

"He kind of says what you said. He thinks being buried in limestone is what kept his insides quiet but able to work. He thinks it might have something to do with the minerals and stuff in limestone. He also thinks the air here isn't good for him. When he was buried, he didn't need to breathe." Shuck notices that Sam's eyes were full of tears. He put his arm around the boy's shoulders. It seemed there was no perfect solution and they were both beginning to realize it.

Chapter 12

By Robodread

Bonnie heard the patio door slide shut indicating the young boy had left. She made her way to the living room to see her dad staring off into space unaware of her entry. He jumped a little when she said, "He seems like a nice kid."

"Yes, he is. I watched him play ball with the other kids, he's a natural." Bonnie smiled to herself. Her dad had been involved in baseball in one way or another for about 60 years. The game would be in his make-up forever, and she was glad. It was good to see him having an interest in someone and something other than her mom. He devoted too much time and energy to caring for her. He was showing signs of fatigue and maybe depression because of his round the clock caregiving. She needed to talk to him about it again.

"Hey dad, you got a minute?" His first thought was to say no and walk outside but he knew there was no point to that. She would say what was on her mind whether it be now, an hour from now or tomorrow. May as well get it over with.

"Sure, honey, what is it?"

"I know how much you love mom and I get that you promised till death do you part, but that didn't refer to being her forever caregiver. I know you will always love her, but mom would want you to look after yourself."

"I am. I can look after her better than anyone else and she would be lost if she left our home. Everything would be strange to her. I have a routine here just like the doctor said."

"I know dad. You are a selfless person and you want to look after her forever. I get that. But I am selfish. I know that my mom is barely the same person I grew up with. It's not your fault or mine that her brain is sick. I am understanding that more and more and I'm beginning to accept it. But I need my dad." Now Bonnie had tears running down her cheeks, but she continued on, "I realize mom's time with us is short, but I want you around for a long time. I can see you are worn out dad. Her being here isn't good for either of you." Now Shuck had tears too. He looked down at his feet knowing what she was saying had some truth to it. "Although no one can love her like you, staying here in the cottage isn't the best thing for her either. In a long-term care home, she will have 24-hour supervision. They have things like lifts to help her into the fancy whirlpool tub. They will work with her to stimulate her brain to help her remain cognitive as long as possible. We won't have to worry about her getting out of the door and wandering off and getting lost or walking into traffic. They have safeguards in place. You won't have to worry about her trying to use the stove while you are in the bathroom or thinking she has to start making dinner and finding the butcher knife."

"I know all those things but putting her there would be like giving up on her."

"No dad it wouldn't. Actually, it would be showing how much you love her-willing to give her the very best care possible. You know you could visit her every day and stay all day if you chose." This was the first time that anything Bonnie had had to say on the subject made sense. Maybe he was just ready to hear it. He did love her enough to want the very best, even if it meant letting go.

"I need to think about," said Shuck quietly, sinking into a chair while wiping his eyes and nose with his hanky.

"I know it's a big decision. I'll be with you all the way; you won't have to deal with it on your own. Mom is down for her nap so I'm going to go dad." She bent down and hugged her dad, holding him tight for a few extra seconds.

Chapter 13

By Robodread

Sam returned from Shuck's house no wiser. Unfortunately, Shuck had no amazing ideas for keeping Camo healthy. He loved his little friend, but he had seen drastic changes in him over the past few weeks. Camo was exhausted all of the time so conversations with him were very short most days. The sun had only kept him able to camouflage for short periods of time-making hiding him very difficult. That meant that Sam couldn't take his buddy with him much. He missed Camo's company and was scared for him. He and Camo had talked about what he should do but Sam wasn't ready to do what needed to be done. Sam plopped down on his bed while Camo who sat buried up to his chest in dust sat in the bottom dresser drawer.

"That you, Sam?"

"Yea."

"I think today has been my worst ever," panted Camo.

"I know, buddy," answered Sam, his voice quivering while silent tears ran down his cheeks. He could see that his friend was now a very pale green color. The dark green skin that he had was now gone and it seemed that no amount of sun was helping.

"Unless I get buried soon, I don't think I can survive." Hearing Camo say it shook Sam up. The threat was real and only he could save the extraordinary animal. But it meant saying good-bye forever. He had never had to say good-bye forever to anyone. How could he do it?

Sam ate very little for supper and was quiet throughout the meal. His mom asked him if he felt sick, but he assured her he was physically fine. There was no doubt that something was bothering her young man, but she wisely let it go. He would talk if, and when, he was ready. So, although it was unusual, mom had no problem allowing Sam to go to Shuck's when he asked.

Sam sprinted the three minutes to the old man's backyard. He could see lights on inside the house but when he gently tapped on the patio door there was no response. He remembered Shuck didn't always hear well, so he knocked harder. After a few seconds, he saw movement inside. Assuming it was Shuck in the shadows, Sam let himself in and came face to face with Nella. She shrieked and began clubbing Sam with her fists. She had little strength, so her blows didn't cause him any pain but instinctively he reached out to grab her fists with one hand while protecting his face with the other. This only made her scream more. Suddenly, Shuck appeared from down the hall and moved as quickly as he could to subdue his wife.

"It's okay Nella, he's a friend, he's a friend, he's a friend," Shuck kept repeating the same phrase in a quieter and quieter voice while leading Nella to a chair. The outburst had left her breathless as well as exhausted and she slumped into the chair putting her face in her hands. "It's alright Nella, you didn't know. I'll bet he scared you, didn't he?" She looked up, still trembling, "Oh, now I see. It's one of Bonnie's school friends-I'm terribly sorry."

"No dear, not one of Bonnie's friends, it's the young man I introduced you to the other day. It's Sam." There was no recognition in her face as having seen Sam only days before. Sam had not moved an inch since the attack and had no idea what to say so he said nothing.

"I want to go to bed. Please take me to bed. I'm so tired. I need to go to bed. I want to go to bed."

"Have a seat, Sam. I'm so sorry about all this. I'm just going to tuck her into bed and I'll be right back." Sam walked to the living room and sat in one of the comfy rockers. He was still processing what had happened when Shuck returned. "I'm so sorry, Sam. I was getting her pills ready when you must have knocked. I didn't hear you, but Nella must have. I've never seen her violent like that before but from what I've read about dementia it's just a natural part of her condition."

"She didn't hurt me, she just scared me a bit."

"She would never act like this if she was healthy. She has always been a sweet, loving lady; but this disease changes a person's personality, so I am learning. She is tucked in bed now so we can visit for a while."

"I came to ask you about Camo. We talked today and he

thinks if he isn't buried in limestone soon, he will die." The tears were once again in Sam's eyes.

"I think he would know best. You know there is lots of limestone around here. There are several quarries within a few minutes by car."

"I know. My mom and I went to the cement plant when I needed limestone dust for Camo when I first got him."

"The cement plant uses lots of limestone. That was good thinking. The one quarry is now a swimming pool but the other one is still in its natural state. It has a walking path next to it.

"Do you think Camo needs to go to one of these?"

"Son, I think if you don't want his life to end you are going to have to. It might give him another chance in another ten, hundred or thousand years from now whenever he is dug up again. But I think it should be Camo's decision. He should decide whether to spend the rest of his life with you or become buried to preserve his life for another time." Sam had thought about little else lately and Shuck wasn't telling him anything he hadn't already thought of. His mind had been very mixed-up about the whole thing but hearing it from Shuck made it seem like good sense. "You know, Sam, I wonder if you don't bury him again and he dies, how will you feel then?" Sam hadn't thought about that angle. He tried to put himself in that position and it felt horrible. He would be responsible for killing Camo. No way could he do that! "This is a very important decision for someone as young as you to make."

"My mom sometimes says we have to do things for the

greater good. She says it's not always what we want but what's best for others. I guess this is something like that."

"Your mom is very wise to have taught you that and you are a very mature young man to understand it and realize that this is one of those times." Sam wiped a tear away with the back of his hand.

"I gotta go," he said suddenly, embarrassed by his emotions. The sliding glass door closed behind him and with more tears he slowly made his way home to Camo. Once home, he crawled into bed knowing he would have trouble getting to sleep. Camo heard Sam come into the room.

"You there, buddy?"

"Yes," came a faint answer.

"I just got back from Shuck's and we think you have to make the final decision. It's your life."

"It's not an easy one for me either," said Camo. "I have grown to like the 21st century, not to mention you and Shuck."

"What was it like when you were buried before?"

"I don't know because I was in a deep sleep then."

"I guess it was like when they put me to sleep to fix my broken arm," reasoned Sam.

"The limestone will preserve me, so I don't decay. Somehow it puts me into a deep sleep. While I'm in that state I don't need to breathe but my heart and other things keep working."

"That sounds a little like how some animals and fish hibernate in the winter. They go into a deep sleep and only wake up again when it's warm. They don't need food or water or anything while in hibernation."

"That sounds like how it is for me."

"That doesn't sound so bad I guess."

"I can't talk now, no energy." Seeing how quickly Camo lost his energy, Sam knew the decision he had to make. He would sleep a little better now.

Chapter 14

Once again, Camo needed to remain buried in his dust. He was too weak to be out of it for any length of time. Sam went off to school anxiously waiting to get back home to see Shuck. Eventually, after what seemed to be an extra-long day, Sam made it home. He quickly checked on his pal then made a bee-line to Shuck's house. He couldn't stop to play at the lot as he had serious business to discuss. Shuck was already sitting on his patio with a warm jacket on and his hands wrapped around a steaming cup of coffee. "Despite the cold, it looks like the kids are picking ball teams. What are you doing here? Aren't you going to play?"

"No Shuck, I've made a decision."

"Okay then. Sit down and let's hear about it."

"I talked to Camo last night and he needs to be buried. I thought being buried sounded really terrible until Camo explained it better. It's really like hibernating-like bears do. When he goes into a deep sleep his body doesn't need any food and stuff. The only difference with Camo is that the limestone will bring him back his strength and make him healthy again and instead of sleeping for a few months, he will sleep for thousands or millions of years."

"And you're okay with this?"

"Well, no, I'd rather he lives with me, but I don't want him to die. Will you help me?"

"Of course, how can I help?"

"Can we drive to the limestone and decide where to bury

him? I think we have to do it soon."

"Certainly, I will drive you. Maybe tomorrow when the nurse and Bonnie are here, I can get away. I know my daughter will be glad that I'm leaving the house. Come by after school and we will take a little road trip."

"I'll see you tomorrow."

The following day, school went by quickly. Sam was not anxious for the road trip with Shuck. It would be the beginning of a sequence of events that he didn't want to be part of.

Shuck was waiting for him in his backyard and as Sam approached, he got up from his chair all ready with the car keys in his hand. He placed an arm around Sam's shoulders and the two walked together to the garage near the front of the house. They climbed into the front seat of the car and Shuck backed out of the garage and headed east.

"I think the quarry with the walking path has had the least disturbance. It's very pretty there, it might be the best place. Let's go there first. What do you think?"

"Sounds good," said Sam quietly. It only took ten minutes before Shuck pulled the car into the parking area designated for trail walkers. The path was easy to follow as crushed limestone had been packed down hard. Many different types of trees, shrubs and even some wildflowers grew between the huge limestone boulders. It didn't take Sam long to decide that this quarry was definitely the place for Camo. Around every bend in the trail, a beautiful area came into view. It would be hard to pick a spot because there were so many that seemed perfect. Seeing the beauty and all the limestone made Sam feel more at peace about the decision. "How will we be able to bury him? This rock is so hard."

"We will bring a few tools. Don't worry we will get it done. There is no one walking now. The sun is setting and it's getting cold out. Around this time of day might be the best time, after all, we don't want anyone observing us and wondering what we are up to. But if we are seen and someone asks us what we are doing we will say we are collecting samples for a school project."

"That sounds good, when?"

"How about tomorrow?" Sam swallowed hard. He hadn't thought about doing it so soon but in his heart, he knew it needed to be done sooner than later.

"Sure," replied Sam, with a lump in his throat.

"Did you see a specific spot, or should we keep looking?"

"I like that area over there. I like that the trees grow near that big rock."

"Okay, that's where we will rest Camo tomorrow. Let's go home." The two began walking back to the car. Two more decisions had been made, when and where. Shuck dropped Sam in front of his house while Sam watched him drive away.

"Where were you? I noticed the kids left the lot quite a while ago," mentioned mom.

"I was with Shuck."

"I'm glad you two have become friends. He is probably a little lonely now that his wife isn't well."

"Yes, he's a nice guy," replied Sam.

"I'm just about to put supper on the table, so wash up."

"I'll be down soon." Sam headed upstairs to check on Camo and tell him the news.

Chapter 15

By Yevgen Kravchenko

Sam awoke dreading the day ahead. He hoped it would go by slowly, yet he knew time was against Camo. The day went by just like any other day. He walked home, changed his clothes then informed his mother that he was spending the next couple of hours with Shuck. With Camo tucked in his dust container safely in his bookbag, he made his way to Shuck's. His aging buddy was once again waiting for him in the backyard.

"Bonnie is with the nurse and Nella, so we have plenty of time. You all set?"

"Yes, Camo is in here," said Sam patting his bookbag gently.

"I have the tools we need already in the trunk. I put them there before anyone came over, to make it easier so I wouldn't have to explain anything to anybody." The drive to the quarry trail was done in silence. Both human occupants had a lot on their minds while the dino just rested, eagerly awaiting his new home. It was nearly sunset by the time the car was parked, the tools rescued from the trunk and they found their way to the spot Sam had picked out. They sat down on a nearby bench, hiding the tools behind them as they waited for a few stragglers to complete their trail walk and head to the parking area. When they were sure they were alone, Sam directed Shuck to the exact spot he wanted to bury his friend. It wasn't too far from the trail nor the bench, yet it was secluded enough that he was sure no one would ever have a reason to tamper with it at least not in this century. He put Camo down on the ground on a slab of limestone to wait until his new home was ready.

"The limestone feels good already," Camo remarked, reassuring Sam he had made the right decision. They kept the dino informed of their progress and occasionally the animal had some directions for them. He wanted it deep enough so no air or water could seep into him. He was sure they were contaminated due to life on earth which had caused his health to fail. Every once in a while, they held him up and shone a flashlight so he could judge their progress for himself. Finally, the moment came to encase the little guy forever. At least it would be forever for Sam. There were some tears. Even Shuck couldn't help but lose a little eye water during the good-byes. Camo snuggled down into his new home thankful to be given a third chance at life. They covered him carefully and built a small hill on top so all water would hopefully run off and not in.

On the way home, Shuck and Sam talked about what had just happened. Sam said it had been easier to do than he thought. Shuck said it was because he knew it was the right thing to do for his beloved buddy. "For the greater good," he reminded Sam. Then he realized tears were running down his cheeks. The tears were not for Sam and not even for Camo but for himself and Nella. By now it was dark and Sam didn't see the sad and tearful face of his elderly friend.

Shuck continued to drive and think. His mind felt more at peace than it had for some time. It was time to talk to Bonnie. Shuck dropped Sam off at his front door. He was dirty from digging and he knew his mom would order him straight into the shower. He could hear his mom and Emily in the kitchen. He yelled that he was home before anyone could catch sight of his filthy face, hands and clothing. In his room, he opened his bookbag and removed the container of dust that Camo had spent so much time in. He carefully placed it on a shelf in his closet. It would always be a reminder of his incredible friend, a miracle from the past. He stepped into the shower and turned on the water; then the tears began. He felt better once he dried off, blew his nose, put on clean clothes and joined his family for supper.

"What were you and Burt doing today?" asked his mom.

"We went to the walking trail by the quarry."

"Oh, it's so nice there, I haven't walked that trail in years."

"I think we might go again sometime," hoped Sam. Anyone walking on the trail or sitting on the bench would be close to Camo. Sam had wanted it just that way!

Chapter 16

Zhanna Millionnaya

Shuck drove into his garage and wiped away his tears before entering the house. Nella and Bonnie were in the living room with the television on, watching a favorite game show. One look at her dad told Bonnie that something was wrong.

"Dad, are you okay?" But she knew he wasn't. His red, puffy eyes were a giveaway.

"I'm okay. I'm okay," he replied, waving her off as he sighed heavily while sitting down in his chair. He looked lovingly at Nella who seemed not to notice his entrance.

"What is it dad?"

"I think we need to talk about a long-term care home for mom."

"Really? I'm surprised. What has made you change your mind?"

"Oh, a lot of things." He wasn't in the mood to go into detail. He couldn't tell her about how encouraging Sam to do the right thing for Camo had made him see that he needed to follow his own advice. He didn't want to tell her that her mom had become aggressive towards Sam the other day or that he really was completely exhausted from caring and worrying about his wife. Instead, he just admitted that she would be cared for better there than he could do at home, even with the extra help he was getting.

"Oh dad, I know how hard this is for you. It is for me too, but it's the right decision for all of us, especially mom." Shuck smiled a little and patted her hand. "Some of my friends have recommended a few places. How about I set up a couple visits for the three of us?"

"That's a good idea, Bonnie."

"There is some supper in the oven for you, dad. I ate with mom earlier."

"You go on home, dear, I'm fine. I'll eat something in a while. Let me know what places you find and I'll do a little research on my end too."

"I'll be off then. Have a good night mom and dad."

A few days later Shuck, Nella and Bonnie toured several long-term care facilities. All were clean, seemed to be well staffed and had private rooms. All of them had special dementia units which they agreed would be the safest and most appropriate for Nella. Shuck thought choosing one would be difficult until while touring the last one, Nella made herself at home and sat right down to help a resident with a jigsaw puzzle. With sincerity, she looked from the puzzle at her husband and daughter and told them to get along home and that she was busy. They looked at each other and smiled. Nella had made the choice herself! In fact, she was not pleased when they told her she couldn't stay but settled down after they promised that she could return once she packed her suitcases.

As Shuck walked out of the long-term care home, he felt incredible relief. It didn't seem like there would be a fuss from Nella about leaving home. They had decided on a facility and he wouldn't be arguing any longer with Bonnie. And as a bonus he would have much needed uninterrupted sleep and be better able to care for himself. Life was changing and he could see it was more positive than negative. He learned he could visit his wife any time and even share meals with her. He or Bonnie could take Nella out for a day or take her home occasionally if they wanted to. It would take a while for him to remember his wife wasn't in a hospital or rehab but in a new home where she would be treated like a resident, not a patient. He knew Nella wasn't the only one who would need to adjust to a different lifestyle- he would too.

"I can't believe your mother's reaction to that last place. I was sure she would be so frightened and you and I would not want to place her there. But she threw us a real curve ball. I feel so much better about everything now."

"I know dad, I feel exactly the same!"

Chapter 17

By Annika Gandelheid

TEN YEARS LATER

Sam pulled into the driveway then retrieved his suitcases out of the trunk along with a large bag of dirty laundry. While opening the back door he yelled, "Hey Mom, you here?"

"Hi Sam, you're home already, you made good time."

"Well, you know how fast people drive on the highway, one has to keep up with the traffic."

"No! One does not! One could obey the speed limit," his mom shot back.

"Yea, I know."

"But I am glad you are home, just the same."

"Where is Em?"

"She is at work and won't be home all evening. She is taking as many part time hours as they will give her. She is saving for a car you know."

"Oh, I know! She seems to think she should have one when she goes back to university. But parking is such a problem on campus. I think she will end up leaving it at home-if she ever saves up enough to buy one."

"You can have that conversation yourself with your sister. How is school going?"

"It's going okay. Maybe a little tougher than I thought it would be. I assumed geology and anthropology would go well together and they do, but my classes sure keep me busy. A double major is a lot of work."

"You got this. Ever since you were a little boy, you have been fascinated with the earth and what has been on it, especially millions of years ago. It was no surprise when you chose to study it formally at university. You are already halfway through, maybe the toughest is behind you. You should go out back and look at the lot. Since you've been home last, the same developer who bought up the senior cottages and built the senior high-rise finally finished putting in the park.

Sam sprinted across the yard and opened the rear gate. What he saw was spectacular! There were no more weeds and dirt but instead, a beautiful lush carpet of soft, green grass. There were no more kids' jackets thrown on the ground to mark the bases but a real ball diamond, actually, two of them, each with their own backstop. There were soccer nets and several basketball hoops cemented into areas of asphalt. At one end, was a jungle gym for little kids. What a transformation! Although kids growing up in the neighborhood now would never know the fun that they had had in the lot they would to be able to enjoy an amazing green space. He also noticed several park benches scattered around the park's perimeter. In fact, one of them was close to his gate. Sam walked up to the new seat and sat down. Then he noticed an engraved plaque attached to the back. It read,' In memory of Camo-from his friends.' Tears welled up in Sam's eyes. He knew Shuck had placed the bench in honor of their secret friend.

Sam heard the latch on his back gate open. His mom walked over to him and sat on the bench too." I don't know who Camo is, but Burt must have thought a lot of him to pay for this tribute." She placed her arm around Sam's shoulders, "I know you miss Burt and you had no way of coming back from your dig in Argentina for his funeral. Burt would have been the first to understand. After the funeral, Bonnie dropped by and gave me a box for you. It's up on your bed."

"Mom, would I have time before supper, to go to the cemetery and pay my respects to Shuck?"

"Of course, take all the time you need." Sam drove to the cemetery and eventually found Shuck's grave. It was a humble headstone much like the great man he had come to know. Over the years, Shuck had played hours upon hours of catch with Sam. He had tutored him on swinging a bat and more importantly, instilled the necessity of learning how to win and lose; lessons he had taken with him for life. It was because of Shuck's coaching that Sam had been given a baseball scholarship to university. He had no interest in playing ball professionally, but Shuck had seen more than a good player in Sam, and he was right. He was growing into a good man and citizen. Sam sat down near the grave and told Shuck about university, the girls he had been dating and all about his dig experience in Argentina. When he had said all he had to say, he drove home.

Following supper, Sam made his way to his room, eager to unpack. The box his mom had mentioned sat in the middle of his bed. He stripped back the packing tape and peered inside. There was an old ball glove and a rookie baseball card, signed by the player himself. Sam knew the glove was the one that Shuck used to catch the ball that denied Willie Stargell a home run. The glove and the card were likely worth money, but he would never let them go. No one would ever know the true bond between himself and Shuck. Just like no one would know who had placed a handful of unshucked peanuts on the great ball player's grave.

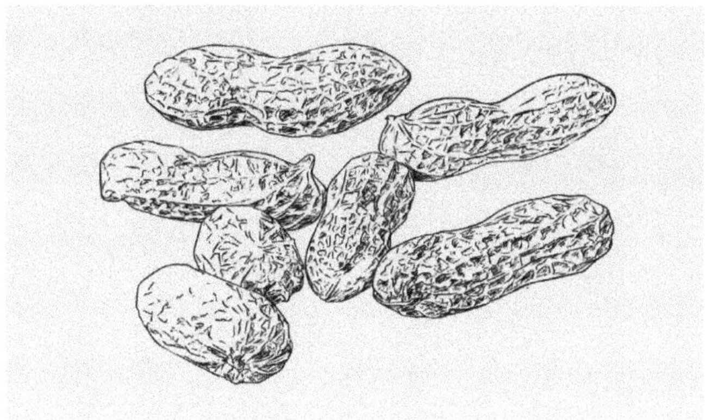

By Kirpmun

Title: *Beads of Courage*®
(Oliver's Story)
- Author: Rosanna Gartley
- Publisher: TotalRecall Publications, Inc.
- Paper Back: ISBN: 9781590952269
- eBook: ISBN: 9781590952320
- Number of pages: 60
- Publication Date: April 25, 2017

Baby Oliver's life started out precariously in the neonatal intensive care unit. Each day, while he was a patient, his parents were given beads of various shapes and colors. Each bead symbolized a medical procedure that Oliver had endured on that day. By the time Oliver was discharged, his collection of beads was impressive.

As Oliver grew, his Beads of Courage® continued to hang on his bedroom wall. Not only were they a reminder of what he had lived through but also served as an inspiration for future challenges.

You won't want to miss what happens during a family vacation when this amazing little boy employs Disney magic to help those who need a little courage.

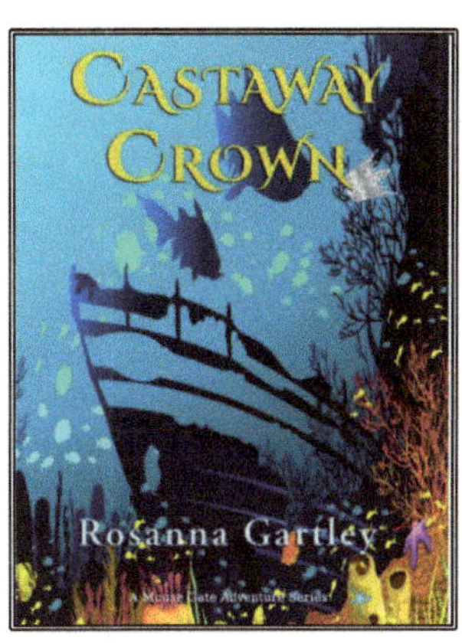

Title: *Castaway Crown*
(Matthew and Anna's
Undersea Adventure)
- Author: Rosanna Gartley
- Publisher: TotalRecall Publications, Inc.
- Paper Back: ISBN: 9781590953327
- eBook: ISBN: 9781590953358
- Number of pages: 68
- Publication Date: April 25, 2017

Matthew and Anna are full of excitement when they learn their family is going on a Disney cruise. With the magic of Disney both children are propelled into an adventure far below the ocean as they are asked to help the sea creatures get rid of a bothersome ghost. With Matthew's above average intellect coupled with Anna's amazing drawing abilities they solve the two-hundred-year-old mystery bringing peace to the sea and the ghost.

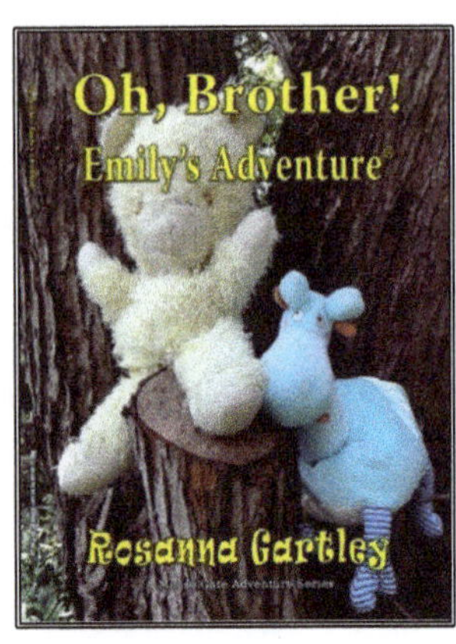

Title: *Oh, Brother!*
(Emily's Adventure)
- Author: Rosanna Gartley
- Publisher: MouseGate.com
- Paper Back: ISBN: 9781590953990
- eBook: ISBN: 9781590954003
- Number of pages: 70
- Publication Date: October 28, 2017

Emily, an only child adored by her parents, finds her life turned upside down and backyards when her parents welcome into their home, Adam, a foster child. Mayhem, mystery and adventure ensue following an enchanted experience that begins during a family vacation to the Magic Kingdom. Disney magic enables Emily to visit the past and the future, allowing her to choose a path altering the lives of her loved ones.

Title: *The Quill Lakes'*
Catastrophe

(Ayden's Adventure)

- Author: Rosanna Gartley
- Publisher: MouseGate.com
- Paper Back: ISBN: 9781590953549
- eBook: ISBN: 9781590953556
- Number of pages: 92
- Publication Date: March 6, 2018

Eleven-year-old Ayden has lived on a farm near the Quill Lakes all his life. When the lakes' flooding puts his family at risk of losing their livelihood and way of life, something must be done. Ayden connects with some uniquely talented forest creatures, uses an ample dose of Disney Magic and relies on his own ingenuity to solve his community's water-logged problem.

Title: *Itchy Feet*
(Miranda and Riley's Adventure)
- Author: Rosanna Gartley
- Publisher: MouseGate.com
- Paper Back: ISBN: 9781590952603
- eBook: ISBN: 9781590952771
- Number of pages: 125
- Publication Date: April 2018

Sisters, Riley and Miranda are beyond excited to tour Disneyland, California. While they are enchanted with the attraction It's A Small World, Disney Magic cocoons them transporting the girls back to the time of American slavery. In the woods near their home, the pair stumble upon an unusual campsite and place their own needs and safety aside to help the humble family they have discovered. Because of the sisters' loving hearts and generosity, combined with a healthy dose of Disney Magic, the Birdsong family finds its way to freedom.

Title: *Curve Balls*
(Sam's Adventure)
- Author: Rosanna Gartley
- Publisher: MouseGate.com
- Paper Back: ISBN: 9781648831683
- eBook: ISBN: 9781648831690
- Number of pages: 96
- Publication Date: May 2022

Sam and his family enjoy a vacation to Disney World where he is thrilled to experience a new ride, The Dino-Soar. This 10- year- old has forever loved everything prehistoric so it's no surprise when he chooses a dinosaur as a souvenir of his trip. Once home, he finds that his keepsake is more than he bargained for. No longer is the plastic figure just a toy. Sam keeps the dinosaur's powers to himself until his elderly neighbor accidently learns the secret. The young boy and the old man have much to learn about each other and their friendship helps both of them make some tough, life-changing decisions.

Authors Bio

Inspiration for Rosanna's children's books comes from her family and friends. A mother of four adult children, four adult bonus kids, and 15 grandchildren, she enjoys placing real-life incidents and characters into her stories. A retired nurse practitioner, Rosanna, originally from the Canadian prairies now resides in southwestern Pennsylvania with her husband, John, and their small dog, Molly.